Sue and the Music Show

The Sound of Long U

by Cecilia Minden and Joanne Meier · illustrated by Bob Ostrom

Published by The Child's World®
1980 Lookout Drive
Mankato, MN 56003-1705
800-599-READ
www.childsworld.com

The Child's World®: Mary Berendes, Publishing Director
The Design Lab: Design and page production

Library of Congress Cataloging-in-Publication Data
Minden, Cecilia.
  Sue and the music show : the sound of long U /
by Cecilia Minden and Joanne Meier ; illustrated
by Bob Ostrom.
    p. cm.
  ISBN 978-1-60253-419-3 (library bound : alk. paper)
  1. English language—Vowels—Juvenile literature.
  2. English language—Phonetics—Juvenile literature.
  3. Reading—Phonetic method—Juvenile literature. I. Meier,
Joanne D. II. Ostrom, Bob. III. Title.
  PE1157.M568 2010
  [E]—dc22   2010005615

Printed in the United States of America in Mankato, MN.
July 2010
F11538

NOTE TO PARENTS AND EDUCATORS:

The Child's World® has created this series with the goal of exposing children to engaging stories and illustrations that assist in phonics development. The books in the series will help children learn the relationships between the letters of written language and the individual sounds of spoken language. This contact helps children learn to use these relationships to read and write words.

The books in this series follow a similar format. An introductory page, to be read by an adult, introduces the child to the phonics feature, or sound, that will be highlighted in the book. Read this page to the child, stressing the phonic feature. Help the student learn how to form the sound with her mouth. The story and engaging illustrations follow the introduction. At the end of the story, word lists categorize the feature words into their phonic elements.

Each book in this series has been carefully written to meet specific readability requirements. Close attention has been paid to elements such as word count, sentence length, and vocabulary. Readability formulas measure the ease with which the text can be read and understood. Each book in this series has been analyzed using the Spache readability formula.

Reading research suggests that systematic phonics instruction can greatly improve students' word recognition, spelling, and comprehension skills. This series assists in the teaching of phonics by providing students with important opportunities to apply their knowledge of phonics as they read words, sentences, and text.

The letter u makes two sounds.

The short sound of **u** sounds like **u** as in: *mud* and *up*.

The long sound of **u** sounds like **u** as in: *cute* and *tube*.

In this book, you will read words that have the long **u** sound as in: *music, blue, fruit,* and *juice.*

Sue is in a show.

Her class practices

many tunes.

The music is so pretty!

Sue wears a blue dress.
She takes her usual place
in line.

The children sing loudly.

They use their best voices.

Their parents clap hands.

"You are great!" they call.

Sue is happy and proud.

"We did it!" Sue says.

After the show the children have a party. There are blue flowers on the table.

The parents and children eat cake. They drink fruit juice. What a treat!

Sue has a huge smile
on her face.

Fun Facts

You probably own a pair of blue jeans, but you might not know that these pants aren't completely blue! Blue jeans typically contain both blue and white threads. Can people be blue, too? If someone says you seem blue, that person is telling you that you look sad. Is your blood blue? No, all human beings have red blood, but someone who comes from a royal family might be described as "blue-blooded."

Are you able to play a musical instrument such as the piano or violin? Wolfgang Amadeus Mozart is one of the world's most famous musicians and lived in the 1700s. Even as a young boy, Mozart enjoyed music. He was playing music when he was four years old and was writing his own music when he was five. Another well-known musician, Ludwig van Beethoven, lived in the late 1700s and early 1800s. Even though Beethoven became deaf, he continued to compose beautiful music.

Activity

Making a Blue Noodle Necklace
Would you like to own a piece of blue jewelry to match your blue jeans? Gather some dry pasta noodles—tube-shaped noodles such as mostaccioli or rigatoni would work best. Paint the noodles blue and let them dry for a few hours. Next, string the noodles along a piece of blue yarn. Tie the ends of the yarn in a knot, and simply place your new necklace over your head!

To Learn More

Books
About the Sound of Long U
Moncure, Jane Belk. *My "u" Sound Box®*. Mankato, MN: The Child's World, 2009.

About Blue
Dumont, Jean-Francois, and Michel Bourque. *A Blue So Blue*. New York: Sterling Publishing, 2005.

Rodrigue, George, and Bruce Goldstone. *Why Is Blue Dog Blue?: A Tale of Colors*. New York: Stewart, Tabori & Chang, 2001.

Stewart, Melissa. *Why Are Animals Blue?* Berkeley Heights, NJ: Enslow Elementary, 2009.

About Music
Aliki. *Ah, Music!* New York: HarperCollins, 2003.

Krull, Kathleen, and Stacy Innerst (illustrator). *M is for Music*. Orlando: Harcourt, 2003.

Thaler, Mike, and Jared D. Lee (illustrator). *The Music Teacher from the Black Lagoon*. New York: Scholastic, 2009.

Web Sites
Visit our home page for lots of links about the Sound of Long U:
childsworld.com/links

Note to Parents, Teachers, and Librarians: We routinely check our Web links to make sure they're safe, active sites—so encourage your readers to check them out!

Long U
Feature Words

Proper Names
Sue

Feature Words with Consonant–Vowel–Silent E Pattern
huge

tune

use

Feature Words with Other Vowel Pattern
blue

fruit

juice

music

usual

you

About the Authors

Cecilia Minden, PhD, is the former director of the Language and Literacy Program at the Harvard Graduate School of Education. She is now a reading consultant for school and library publications. She earned her PhD in reading education from the University of Virginia. Cecilia and her husband, Dave Cupp, live outside Chapel Hill, North Carolina. They enjoy sharing their love of reading with their grandchildren, Chelsea and Qadir.

Joanne Meier, PhD, has worked as an elementary school teacher, university professor, and researcher. She earned her BA in early childhood education from the University of South Carolina, and her MEd and PhD in education from the University of Virginia. She currently works as a literacy consultant for schools and private organizations. Joanne lives in Virginia with her husband Eric, daughters Kella and Erin, two cats, and a gerbil.

About the Illustrator

Bob Ostrom has been illustrating children's books for nearly twenty years. A graduate of the New England School of Art & Design at Suffolk University, Bob has worked for such companies as Disney, Nickelodeon, and Cartoon Network. He lives in North Carolina with his wife Melissa and three children, Will, Charlie, and Mae.